contents

copyright

acknowledgements

thank You, God, for the beautiful, curious mystery of creation,

thank you to Jarrod Taylor for reading numerous early drafts, giving great feedback, taking phone calls at inconvenient times, and helping me wrestle with the difficult themes,

thank you to Sandra Starrett Lee for providing helpful feedback from her experience and education as a counselor,

thank you to the friends who read this who have experienced its themes first hand (i am inspired by your great bravery),

thank you to Anne Batey and her late husband Tom, whose faithfulness to The Lord and to each other inspired a portion of this story,

thank you to Janelle Musick for professionally editing a heavily-stylized, difficult to edit piece, thank you to Jeremie Benzinger for the cover art,

thank you to Donut Country and Starbucks Fortress who gave me space to create, immeasurable kindness, and also coffee and donuts,

thank you to all of my friends and family who have encouraged this and other projects along the way,

and thank you to mom and dad for always, always believing in me.

introduction

this is my second self-published short story. it adheres to the same stylistic choices i made with my first short story, "kindling".

i am a filmmaker, which will no doubt be evident as you read. as a screenwriter, i write what can be seen and heard. i adapt that practice to my prose as well.

i am a very internal and emotional person, and the style of writing here attempts to reach the deep emotions of the reader. i borrow from formal conventions, but do not feel required to adhere to them. i try to do what i think serves the story best.

i care less about how you enjoy the story and more about what you do with it. i pray it might prompt you to pick up the phone and call someone you love. i pray it may give you the courage to tell your story so that someone else in the darkness finds a hand to hold on to. i pray it helps you understand what some people feel in the darkness. i pray you notice — really notice — the other human beings around you, that you are kind to them, that you listen to them, that you love them in ways that are appropriate and helpful.

and if you are in the darkness, i pray you know that you are not alone.

Godspeed.

the darkness rolled over her

in the time it takes you to read this story,
8 Americans will commit suicide.

friday night

"God, kill me."

it was a genuine prayer. it always had been. Guin lay on her back, not moving, the gruesome cold darkness pushing her shoulders into the bed. the weight of its assault pressed her whole body into the mattress. she searched the ceiling, beyond the ceiling, for rescue. its ice cold grip laced its fingers around her throat, choking out air, choking out life. inside her, emptiness and loneliness rumbled through her gut like vicious hunger. like a crashing wave into a craggy pit, the darkness rolled over her. stronger, colder, and heavier. filling her emptiness like acid, making the nothing inside her bigger and worse than before, scraping out the chasm inside her wider and deeper. the more the darkness roiled, the less it seemed it would end.

if the gravity would lift, if the pain would stop, if the darkness would recede, even for a moment, i could get out of bed, Guin thought. kickstart something new. anything. just move, just try.

but she could not. and so, the prayer.

she looked at the clock. 3:27am. her alarm would sound in an hour. she intended to exercise, but she already knew she would just keep hitting snooze for an hour until the last minute.

the last minute. the last trip. the last time with these girls. they were the only people in the world that even remotely cared about her. otherwise, she would not have set the alarm. on the nightstand next to the clock was a bottle of sleeping pills. after this last goodbye, she would return home, take the whole bottle, and never wake up.

everything was arranged. she'd had a will for some time. she'd sent her cat to her aunt's. her aunt loved cats, and she knew that after it was over, she'd be good there. she'd even arranged to be found. Mrs. Hiddlemeyer next door had been a terrible neighbor. it seemed like every time Guin went out, she had all kinds of nosy questions and always knew what everyone else in the neighborhood was doing. why didn't she just mind her own business? Guin could always see her grey eyes plotting something behind those pop-bottle glasses of hers. she'd pretend to be nice, as many Southern women do, but underneath the surface was a murky layer of hostility and judgement. even so, Mrs. Hiddlemeyer would often collect mail when Guin was out of town, that sort of thing. so it wasn't a request that was out of place. yet, Guin felt no guilt about having her be the one to discover her. if anything, a twinge of sick pleasure in it.

the only thing she'd really left open-ended was a job interview on Monday her friend Kathleen had arranged for her. Kathleen had tried to be sympathetic with Guin, but much of her advice hurt more than helped. she was well-meaning, but Kathleen's opinions showed she had no idea what it was like for Guin, making Guin feel even more isolated. still, everything Guin had earned and saved during her short time in the army years ago was long gone. Guin had been subsisting off of her settlement with her ex-husband and some disability. but just subsisting. and more than needing money, Guin needed a new life. on this point, Kathleen and Guin agreed, and so Guin agreed to the interview.

but in recent days, she was drowning in darkness. her whole life, certainly the last few decades, had been a constant cycle of being pulled under and crushed, then struggling, searching for sun above the surface, where the air is. but whatever light may shine distantly above her had grown dim until it had disappeared completely. no more energy to swim through it, no more breath, no warmth in the abyss, fathoms of pressure pushing her deeper to the bottom. a new job wouldn't change this. this would be forever. she had prayed and prayed to God to take her, but if He was there, He remained silent. so she decided to do it herself. she hoped bailing on the interview wouldn't cause problems for Kathleen somehow. if it did, Kathleen surely could say why, and people would purse their lips and nod, as if they understood.

Guin reached over and grabbed a pencil from her nightstand, slipping it into the brace on her arm to scratch an itch but wasn't able to reach it. she got up and threw her sling over her neck, carefully placing her braced arm into it. a deep breath later, she was up, and started putting a few personal things into a small duffle bag with her free hand.

her small bag packed, she shuffled into the kitchen and began brewing some coffee. as the percolator began to pop, she looked at the dishes in the sink. she thought about rinsing them and putting them in the dishwasher, but why bother. she drifted slowly through the house, watering the plants. they had been the only ones, it seemed, to always be there for her. even the cat would often rather be left alone. but the plants, they never went anywhere, they only required water and sun, and they didn't even ask for that. in return, they breathed in her bitter air and purified it. she would often press her face into one of her potted plants and breathe deeply, praying she could exhale all of the darkness. praying the big flat leaves would reach up and touch her face and hold her, breathing light and warmth back into her. it was a lot to demand of a house plant. but she loved them. watering them seemed as futile as everything else, but she figured someone else might love them.

back in the bedroom, she carefully unlatched the velcro on the brace about her wrist. she lightly scratched the days-old itch, then cleaned her arm with a wet wipe and replaced the brace and sling.

the alarm sounded. she turned it off. she slipped off her robe, laying it across the bed. on her phone, she pulled up her workout app, then closed it and headed for the shower.

saturday morning

all of the women were gathered around the van as Guin pulled into the church parking lot. this trip had become an annual trek for most of the crew. two years ago, it was horse riding with an organization geared toward helping people manage PTSD. last year had been an art therapy retreat. since few in the group possessed artistic ability, that trip ended up being more frustrating than calming. so this year, they were headed back outdoors, this time to the mountains. this organization, Current Healing, was geared specifically to Veterans, and the program was designed to take them out of their day-to-day life and teach them the calming art of fly fishing in the rivers of the East Tennessee mountains.

Guin had no interest in fly-fishing, so when she first heard of it, she dismissed it. but a woman she had served with, Cynthia, had been several times and talked her into it. Guin liked the outdoors; that's one thing that had drawn her to the military to begin with. and it sounded peaceful and relaxing, which was something that mattered to her months ago when she'd agreed to go along. but she mainly accepted the invitation to be around

Cynthia. even as Guin's darkness had recently swallowed her, set like concrete within her, she kept her word and came. none of them lived close to each other, but even so, Guin had built a rapport with these ladies, as they all understood something about each other that no one else seemed to. she hadn't seen Cynthia since last year, so this was really the only opportunity to say goodbye.

Cynthia's PTSD was from the war. they had served together, but Cynthia saw action. Guin had mostly been helping build infrastructure where she served, and never saw any real danger. she heard a lot about it, but Cynthia had lived it. Cynthia would tell Guin stories of waking up in the middle of the night, shouting, frightening her whole family. but her husband was an understanding and patient man, and they were able to find a way through it.

leading the group was a large, quiet woman named Susan. Susan was now the group organizer, but had been a recipient of their care in the past. she was a kind, meek woman who led the group like a den mother. she was always prepared, always respectful, and called everyone 'dear'. Guin parked near the church sign at the end of the lot and tried to quietly join the others. Susan was already going over the itinerary for the day.

"... then back at the campsite tonight, we'll have a fish fry with some other food. we will cook together with the boys, and if you haven't been, well, it's a hoot!"

Guin felt Maxine glare at her as she joined the group. Maxine had a flattop and was built like a tractor. her personality was equally subtle. Max pointed to her watch, a cheap silver piece that was meant to be decorative but instead looked like it might cut off the circulation in her ham-hock wrist.

"thought we might have to leave without you!"

a few of the other ladies turned and looked at Guin. Cynthia made a face at Max, who ignored it.

"sorry i'm late."

"that's okay, dear. you haven't missed anything." Susan winked at Guin. "okay, ladies, let's load up and hit the road."

even submerged in darkness, Guin found some delight in the road trip. Cynthia always had funny stories. the two ladies in front of them, Linda and Danielle, listened and laughed as they knitted. if they could just do this for a few hours, she thought, it will be a pleasant note to go out on.

another woman, Samantha, leaned against the window, her head on a wadded up jacket, sleeping. Guin watched her sleep. she could see the darkness over her, too. she wondered if Sam really slept, or if she pretended as to avoid everyone. if not for her fondness of Cynthia, Guin would probably be asleep, too.

Sam was young. too young for darkness. Guin was 48. most of the things life had to offer had come and gone, she felt. but for Sam — she couldn't be more than 25 — there was so much light left for her to find. wasn't there?

the van's tires crunched across the gravel parking lot in front of the old store and came to a stop. Guin peered past Cynthia through the window. gathered around the bed of an old pickup were half a dozen men, most of them old. they looked exactly how you might expect, a bunch of old farts in bad jeans and thick shoes sharing who knows what kind of stories or jokes. the bed of the truck had an assortment of camping supplies, most of which looked older than Guin, she thought. the store was like something out of the background of a Norman Rockwell painting. in the

7

window were fishing reels and beer ads, and a hand-made sign that read "live cricket's".

the girls got out of the van, becoming suddenly sheepish in the presence of the men. even Maxine managed to be quiet. the men got quiet,too, but wore big, welcoming smiles. Susan stood between them, waving the women closer.

"well ladies, we're going to make a quick pit stop here, then we'll follow the gentlemen to their campsite where you'll get to meet your fly fishing mentor for the day. it's about a twenty-minute drive, so grab a bottle of water or use the restroom, and then we'll get back on the road."

Guin stood in the back of the group of women. she turned to see Sam sidling up behind her. "you okay?"

"yeah," Sam said, "just tired i guess." she squinted in the sun as she looked around. "i'm kind of a city girl. i'd rather be at an art show or something."

"you ever done this before?"

"no. you?"

"nope. we did horse riding a couple of times. but the girls are kinda fun. and it'll be relaxing if you let it."

Sam just nodded and kept looking around, mostly to avoid eye contact, Guin figured.

"one time we did art therapy. maybe you can ask for that next time." Sam scratched her elbow. "do you paint or anything?"

"nope."

"well. that's okay. most of us were pretty terrible."

Sam moved the gravel around with her shoe. Guin abandoned it.

"i just like to look at it," Sam said eventually. "there's a college near my house. sometimes i'll go over there and, you know. just look."

"you have friends over there?"

"i mean. i know a few of them." Guin waited for more, but. that was it.

"you want to get a soda or something?" Guin didn't really want anything, but she wanted to keep Sam engaged in what was going on, and small talk didn't seem to be doing anything for either of them.

"uh... sure."

they stepped around the other ladies to head inside. one of the old men leaned on the back of a pickup. he had a wide-brim hat, a thick beard, a flannel shirt, and chest-high waders. "how y'un's doin?"

"fine, thanks." Guin squeezed out a polite smile. she'd hoped for something kinder or warmer to respond with, but she wasn't much for talking to anyone any more. besides, it was more than Sam said, which was nothing.

inside, Guin got a bottle of water, mostly to justify having gone inside. Sam opted not to get anything. she said she'd changed her mind, but Guin assumed she just didn't want to be left alone. why she picked Guin to shadow was a mystery, though.

soon the women were back in the van. they fell in line behind the old men's trucks, and the small caravan wound its way up River Road.

§

the old men's campsite was already set up. it looked like these guys knew what they were doing and had been there for at least a few days already. Guin felt a little intimidated by it. she didn't like being in situations where she didn't know what was going on, where she didn't have some measure of control. especially if there was an older man telling her what to do. she took a deep breath and thought about last year's art instructor. she couldn't remember the man's name, but he was kind and patient with her. she hoped she'd get someone as nice, polite, and forgettable this year. she pressed on her brace, trying to quell the itch underneath.

Guin stepped out of the van and took a deep breath. it was summer, and the sun was hot on her cheeks. she was surrounded by green trees, dancing in the mountain breeze. the gently swaying limbs wafted fresh oxygen her way, and she drank it in.

as everyone loaded out, Susan began handing out name tags and pairing everyone up. Guin's anxiety began to seep up as she watched everyone greet and shake hands. she brought a small day bag with dry shoes and socks, a change of pants just in case, and a belt pack with her personal stuff in it — money, sanitizer, small first aid kit. she knelt down to dig out the belt pack, hoping it'd be a good enough excuse to not have to shake hands, or explain why she didn't want to.

"Guin, you're with Mr. Roy." it was the man who'd said hello at the store. now she felt even worse about not being more polite, and she was about to be more rude by turning down the expected handshake. she stood, but Mr. Roy just stood there cross-armed.

"hello again." he said, smiling a polite greeting, keeping his hands tucked under his flannel. why didn't he offer a handshake? does he know? did Susan tell him she doesn't like her hands touched? or really to be touched at all? how did that conversation go, she wondered. and when did it happen? how long has he had to judge her, or pity her. Guin's anxiety continued to simmer. these thousand thoughts flashed through her psyche in an instant.

Guin gave a little wave with her free hand. "hi." she bent down again and grabbed the belt pack, rose, and snapped it around her waist.

"Guin has a dog, too, Roy!" Susan said, moving away. she always liked to connect people with things they have in common, but she also could never remember anything.

"actually, i have a cat," Guin said, once Susan was out of earshot.

Roy shrugged. "i have a horse." Guin chuckled, not sure if it was a joke or not. "i got some extra gear in my truck, less'n you got your own."

"nope. i'm a novice."

she followed Roy over to the old pickup. the rusty passenger door opened with a creak, and he folded the seat forward, pulling some gear from behind it.

he assembled his rod and went over all the parts with her — reel, line, leader, flies. he pulled a nail from the bib pocket on his waders and asked how she was at tying knots. she waved her fingers at him from the brace in her sling.

"right." he lifted his hat and scratched his forehead as he look at her immobile arm.

"sorry, i'm kinda handicapped this trip."

"nonsense."

"well, can you fly fish with just one hand?"

"well. i can. but. it's not easy."

"Mr. Roy, i'm mostly here for the fresh air and to see my girlfriends. if all i can do today is just watch you at work, that's fine with me."

"well. that's fine with me, too, then."

Maxine passed by with her mentor, a thick, tan man with high hair. Guin could tell he was loud just looking at him. whoever paired them up had done a fabulous job. he leaned in toward Guin, which caused her to flinch, a reflex she tried her best to control, with little success.

"you got the best fly fisherman up here," he said, loudly, and kept walking. Roy didn't react.

"are you the best?" Guin asked.

Roy wrapped his fly line and clear leader around the nail. "ah... that's Dennis. he owes me money. tryin to get out of it." she wondered if she'd ever get a straight answer from him. he had a dry sense of humor, and was a little cranky, but it was a pretend cranky, which she found to be charming for some reason. he slipped the nail out and pulled the lines tight. the knot was sleek and symmetrical.

"that's beautiful."

"well. t'ain't for lookin at."

Roy was as bad at taking compliments as she was. she was pretty sure they'd get along just fine.

"you ready to get movin?"

"let's do it." and for just a second, Guin found herself having fun.

§

Roy drove so effortlessly through the winding roads and trails, it was clear he'd been coming here for years, probably longer than

Guin had been alive. Roy seemed kind, but thrust two strangers into a car together, and the awkwardness drowns out everything else. Guin wished he'd speak first. finally, he did.

"you were in the military?"

"army. for a little while."

"thank you for your service."

"did you serve?"

"no ma'am, i did not. but i'm thankful for those who did. never forget it."

the truck's rusty exhaust and the tires crunching up the gravel road made small talk difficult. which was fine with Guin; she hated small talk. Roy didn't seem much for it either. so she just stared out the window, filing away the pretty landscapes like postcards in her mind she might want to pull out and look at later. but then, she wouldn't have a later. she turned her attention to the itch in her brace instead.

the truck pulled over, and Roy cut the engine. "we're here."

"already?"

"we'll start here and walk our way up river."

Guin opened her door with a loud creak that offended the serene landscape. the truck was in a small shoulder made presumably for fishermen to pull off and park. next to the truck was a sign nailed to a tree: 'notice to all camper's...'. either the rules of grammar had changed, or there was only one signmaker in this part of the Smokies.

"i didn't bring no snacks or nothin," Roy said. it didn't really sound like an apology.

"i'll be fine."

"i got some bottled water if you wanna haul the backpack around." Roy pulled the pack from the bed of the truck and handed it to her. Guin pretended to scratch her brace.

"yeah, great. just set it there."

Roy set it down and retrieved his fishing gear from the cab. Guin slipped the pack over her shoulder. the banks next to the river tended to be high and thick with brush, but here there was a nice, cleared slope down to the water.

"this spot's a little easier for me to get in," Roy said, rod in hand, shuffling his way down toward the huge rock shelves below. "follow me."

the water was cold and strong. in the summer sun with the peaceful sound, Guin found this surprising. but it pushed against her ankles, buffeting her shins, reminding her she does not belong here, she is a guest. she had bought special pants that would dry quickly, but they were also thin, and she could feel the heat leaving her legs. her socks and shoes squished, soaked in seconds, and she wondered how soon her toes would be wrinkly, how long she could stay in.

"this is also a good spot for us to get started," Roy said, continuing. Guin realized they'd not said a word to each other the whole way down. was that on her? he's the guide, after all. "it's nice and open here. trees crowd in up river."

he fiddled with his rod for a minute, then started pulling line out. he gave it a few quick whips and the line lengthened. within a few minutes, he was gracefully whipping the fly line back and forth. the line sparkled in the sunlight, and lithely slinked through the air above Roy's head, whirring a song for itself to dance to. he let the line fall and reeled it in.

"did you see that?"

"yes, it's beautiful."

"what?" it was clear they weren't talking about the same thing. "did you see what i did with the fly." he pointed toward the water.

Guin had been so busy watching the process, she'd not paid any attention to the fly.

"oh, sorry, no. i missed it."

"well, the fly's the thing. everything is else is just about gettin the fly to that fish. watch it again."

she watched as he whipped back and forth same as before. once the line was long enough, the dry fly on the end of his line paused above the surface of the water before being whipped back. then again, then again. each time it was inches from where it had paused before. how was he able to do this from a good twenty feet away? he cast again, but this time the fly landed on the surface of the water, and Roy began reeling it in.

"your accuracy is amazing."

"just takes practice is all." Roy cast again while they talked. Guin found a flat place to sit down.

"once you land it, how long do you stay there?"

"you don't." Roy landed and started reeling in. "you're a bug. you're on the move. you're alive."

"so what about all these pictures of people with their poles in the water? sitting on the shore with their hat over their eyes?"

"that's bait fishin. bait fishin is different. with fly fishin, you gotta keep movin." Roy grabbed the end of his fly line and pulled it to him. he dried off the fly and hooked it in a guide on his rod. "speakin o'which, don't get too comfortable." and he was off, wading through the current. Guin hopped to her feet and followed after him.

Roy had this fascinating way of navigating the stream. he would heave a leg up and plant the boot of his wader down, then lean his weight over it as he pushed off with the other foot once he was sure he had good footing. it was an odd-looking teeter-tottering, but seemed to really work, every step strategic. and he never misstepped. Guin followed behind him, rock to rock, mimicking his steps and his gait. she quickly found she was able to navigate the strong current and the slippery rocks almost as well as he.

she stepped more quickly as she gained confidence. she took another step, and it faltered. her leg swept from under her across the slimy stone, and she tumbled into the oncoming stream. she yelped. Roy reached for her, grabbing her elbow. another yelp as she yanked her elbow from him, sending her splashing into the water. she looked at him frightened and embarrassed, almost on her back as he stood over her. she felt instinctively vulnerable — on her back, alone under the shadow of a man, in the middle of nowhere — but then she remembered who she was with, and the adrenaline subsided.

Roy frowned, his hand retracted. "sorry, it was... reflex."

"me, too."

but his apology meant that, yes, he did know. and now they were both aware. she caught her breath and tried to let her anxiety wash away with the current, as cold water rushed over her waistband and down her pantleg.

"do you need help?"

what a question. "no, i'm okay." she found a solid place to put her foot and pushed herself up onto all fours. eventually she was able to get a leg under her and stand up. "i got a little arrogant, i guess."

"my waders have felt on the bottom. they help with the slime. sorry, i should have said something."

Guin breathed in, and out. "okay. now what?"

"we keep movin."

"don't want to fish here?"

"well, not any more. we probably scared 'em pretty good. we'll have to go upstream a bit."

"sorry."

"not your fault. it happens. but that's why we walk upstream. whatever you do disturbs everything downstream."

a few more little waterfalls upstream and Roy situated himself with some sure footing. Guin settled in just behind to watch.

"see that dark spot up there? that's a nice deep little hole. might be something hiding in there." Roy whipped a few times, then cast. nothing. he cast again. something struck at the line.

"looky there!"

"i ain't got 'im yet." Roy cast again, another strike as something splashed the surface. Roy gave his rod a whip but came up empty. another cast, and nothing. cast again, nothing.

"let's go."

"you almost had him."

"once you've had a strike or two, they're onto you. best to just move on. let's go." Guin didn't expect this much walking, especially uphill over slimy rocks in ice cold rushing water. she wasn't tiring yet. she was in great shape. but this was like climbing stairs. with wet socks. she snapped out of her thoughts to see Roy about ten feet away from her already, so she hustled to catch up.

once he found a new spot, she watched him cast toward some small rapids. he landed the fly above the tiny waterfall, then let the fly float back with the current.

"sometimes they like to hang out behind a rock facing upstream." Roy continued his masterclass. "they're always facing upstream, waiting for something."

me too, Guin thought.

"so i'm gonna give 'im something." his third cast blooped into the water, cascaded down, then disappeared! Roy whipped his rod, moving only his wrist, setting the hook. "got 'im." Roy reeled him on back, his prey flopping and splashing as he reeled him closer. once his catch was close enough, Roy squatted awkwardly, bending over to grab the fish. he snagged it like the expert he was, hooked his thumb in its mouth, and held it up. it twitched and flippered, slinging water. the sun prismed across its slimy skin, illuminating the iridescent rainbow down its side. it was probably about ten inches. "how bout it?"

"very nice!" Guin always enjoyed watching someone who was excellent at what they do, whatever it was. Roy had a tight smile hidden somewhere under his grey beard, and he slipped the wriggling trout into his creel.

"okay. keep movin."

and up the river they went. Guin mostly watched, and did find herself calming down. not from anything in particular. as she relaxed, she became aware of how tense she had been. for months. years, really. so many little things would remind her of the attack. cortisol and adrenaline would shoot through her body. she could see and hear and feel the toughest moments as if they were happening again. sometimes she'd wake up in bed, fighting. and even when her mind knew the difference, her body didn't. cortisol and adrenaline are a great natural defense, but they never went away, and it had taken a toll on her. despite eating well and exercising, she was always tired, blue, worn out. pain turned to turmoil, and turmoil to darkness. and the longer the darkness lasted, the deeper it settled, making a home in her. but somehow, out here, in the sun, with the white noise of the rolling river, watching Roy's ballet in the air, focused on nothing but the fly... it was hypnotic, and calming. as her psyche rested, her body healed, and the darkness... well, at least it had stopped growing. it's a shame this trip was only once a year. it might have done her some real good otherwise. but it was too late now, anyway.

she couldn't tell if Roy was experiencing the same thing. anyone who is good at something also experiences a great deal of pressure and stress from it. and though Roy was a master fly fisherman, he still dealt with tangled lines, lost flies, ones that got away. but with every snag, he'd adjust his hat and keep heading up river.

hooked on the front of his vest were a menagerie of dry flies, like war medals. different types, two or three of each.

"what's the difference in the flies?"

"well. different times of year, the fish are lookin for different things. when bugs are in the larval stage, you want a grubby-lookin nymph that sinks a little. right now they're into these 'adult' mayflies with the wings. and sometimes i like to use these here with the bright orange."

"what do they look like?"

"they look like a 70-year-old man who can't see well tryin to fish."

Guin chuckled. "do you get upset when you lose one?" she was surprised at herself for striking up conversation, but after the first few hours of mostly silence, she needed a little.

"not really. i have a couple of flies i don't use, though, so's i won't lose 'em." he pulled in his hook, set it in the rod, and waded to her. he pointed at the top row of flies on his vest, their hooks securely in the fabric. "i had been using this one the morning my son was born, so i call it Aaron, after him. these are Harold and Millie, after our dogs."

"you name them?"

"the dogs?"

"the flies."

"sure, why wouldn't i?"

Guin smiled and shrugged.

"and my wife gave me these two on our thirty-fifth anniversary."

"and what'd you name them?"

"Ball, and Chain."

Guin rolled her eyes. Roy gave her a little wink. and then there was this moment, nothing weird. just. if she wasn't careful, she'd make a friend. there was no point in it. her smile disappeared. Roy looked away. "well, i guess i'm done here. let's keep movin."

saturday afternoon

she'd not cared about snacks when they started out, but now her stomach was rumbling. she pulled a water bottle out of the bag.

"Roy, do you want some water?"

he stopped progressing up the rocks and considered it. "probably a good idea, i reckon." he walked back down. she held out a bottle, and he carefully took it from its base, so as not to touch her. he nodded in gratitude, and they broke the plastic seals and took a drink.

"i think i might sit down for a minute, if that's okay," Guin said.

"sure."

she did, but he just stood.

"i'd join you, but i'm liable to not get back up." suit yourself, she thought.

at this point in the day, it was getting hard not to catalog the beauty around her in her memory. they'd just come up a fairly steep area, and it had opened into a beautiful smooth flat spot, like a small lake. there were a few large rocks that crested the surface, giant granite whales breaching for air. some small rapids way up ahead as the river continued its ascent. a mighty hickory bent out from the canopy of smaller trees and reached over the river toward the sun. a large bird soared overhead, throwing its shadow across the landscape below as it passed. a family picnicked on the bank, their blanket spread on a large boulder that jutted out upriver. everything felt frozen in time, but from some time long past, a time she imagined that didn't know the darkness yet. she looked at the plastic water bottle in her hand, and it felt anachronistic. she picked at a corner of the modern label and peeled it away.

"everything up here feels like it's stuck in the 50s or something. but like, in a good way."

"well, i've been comin up here for a long time, and things haven't changed much." Roy squinted up into the sun. "d'you see that?" the large bird slowly floated overhead against the wind.

"hawk?"

"nope." the bird flapped its wings and drifted into the trees, perching on a large limb. Guin could now see its white head.

"that's a bald eagle."

"yup. you ever seen a bald eagle before?"

"no." Guin admired it. having a new experience hadn't occurred to her. no point in filing it away, but she could enjoy it right now for what it was.

"well. now you have." Roy crushed his empty bottle flat, the harsh plastic noise bringing her back into real time. Guin took it from him and put it back in the backpack. she summoned her energy and stood.

"keep moving?"

"actually, this is a good spot for you."

"for me?"

"yes ma'am." Roy held out the rod. she took it in her free hand, but looked at her brace. "don't worry about that. we'll just practice a little motion." he coached her through wrist movement, feeling the motion of the rod, getting that flywheel-style movement just right, back and forth, anticipating the length of the line, firm whips, but not too fast, nice and smooth. as the fly line sizzled past her ear, she smiled, the hair on her neck and arms standing with a girlish glee. her aim was terrible, her ballet more of a clumsy two-step, but she was enjoying it, and getting better.

one cast went way out into the flat pool before them, and the line slacked into a broad artwork of curl. at the end of her line, a small splash and her fly disappeared.

"whoa, you got somethin!" Roy got excited.

"here, take it!" Guin thrust the rod at him.

Roy backed away, "no! set it, reel him in!"

"no, you take it!"

"set the hook!" Roy took a step back. Guin pulled the rod back, too slow, not even taking slack from the line. "harder! you gotta-- pull in the slack!" she tried pulling in line with her braced hand like she'd seen Roy do when casting. "no-- the reel! here lemme see it!"

thank God, she thought, and gladly gave him the rod. Roy's hand brushed hers, but she barely noticed in the frenzy. Roy quickly clicked the reel, pulling in the slack, and then gave it a firm whip.

"i think we got 'im!' splashing at the end of the line confirmed it. Roy handed the rod back. "here, you finish it off."

"no! you do it!"

"it's already set, all you gotta do is reel it in. c'mon now, this is your fish."

she retrieved the rod from him, took a deep breath, and started clicking the wheel. with the brace, it was slow and awkward, but by gum she was fishing! the splashes got closer, and she lifted the rod revealing her catch, a four-inch rainbow trout flittering at the end of the fly line.

"keep him in the water!" she lowered her rod, and the splashing resumed. Roy reached down and pulled the line to him, got him between the gills, and pulled him out.

Guin looked at her catch with a delighted disappointment. "he's so..."

"you couldn't get a whole fishstick outta this one. here." he held the little fish toward her.

"beg your pardon?"

"well i gotta get your picture."

"oh, that's okay."

"nah, come on."

she handed him the rod and slipped her fingers into the fish's mouth and gills, holding it down at her waist, her arm stiffed away from her. Roy pulled out his cell phone from the bib pocket on his waders.

"you gotta hold it up so i can get you both."

she brought it a little closer to her face, where its wriggling splashed her with a cold spritz of river water. Roy snapped the picture and tucked his phone away.

"we'll call it 'Abby'."

"is it a girl?"

" 'Abby Tizer'." Guin groaned, but couldn't help laughing, the whole experience finally over. he stepped over to her and opened his creel. "drop him in."

§

Roy's tires crunched across the gravel as they pulled into the store parking lot where they'd first met. this time, it was just the two of them.

"i gotta hit the head."

Guin laughed to herself and got out to stretch.

"you want somethin to eat? it'll be a few hours before dinner."

that sounded like a good idea. "sure."

Roy shuffled back to the bathrooms. Guin eyeballed the conveniences around her, certain many of them bore product labels from the 80s. can dish soap go bad? some items were curious; who suddenly needs pantyhose up here? there was a small bottle of sleeping pills. just one. not her brand. small bottle. too small. she'd done her research. and did people really have trouble sleeping up here?

she grabbed a granola bar from a basket beside the counter. next to the register was a display case of flies, probably about 60, every one of them unique, beautifully decorated. slipped into the top of the case was a large notecard: "Miller Custom Fly's". guess we found our sign-maker, she thought.

"did you do this?" the clerk peered over his reading glasses as she motioned toward the card.

"nope, your friend Roy ties those flies himself."

"no, i meant the... wait, that Roy?" she pointed toward the bathroom.

"Roy Miller." it was only now she realized she'd never asked his full name. she felt like that was rude, even though she suspected she'd never see him again after today. the clerk walked over and lifted the plexiglass lid to the fly case. "best flies on North River. probably the best east of the Mississippi. we have a lot of people that drive from all over just to pick up a few. a lot of these in the case are just kindly to look at, but we keep the more useable ones on the rack." he thumbed to a pegboard behind him with smaller, duller flies in little baggies. there were hundreds.

she leaned in close to the flies in the display. each had a tiny price tag tied to it. some were $15 or more. "they're more expensive than i thought."

"crook marks em up too high," Roy said, shuffling up behind her. the clerk shut the lid.

"he oughta sell em for double. people'd pay it."

"really?" Guin was genuinely surprised this old coot spent his time making these delicate masterpieces, that he was in demand for miles around, some kind of celebrity.

"he just says that 'cause he's paid on percentage." Roy set down two glass bottles of RC Cola and two Moon Pies.

"you catch anything today, Roy?"

"ah, buncha limbs, two boots, and a tire." Roy grabbed Guin's granola bar and tossed it back. Guin put her hand on her hip. "fishermen don't eat granola." Guin rolled her eyes.

"better not let the warden catch you. you know one's the limit on them boots."

"the heck am i gonna do with one boot? gimme a six-pack of Budweiser, too." as the clerk walked back to the cooler behind the counter, Roy looked at Guin and tapped on the plexiglass case. "pick you one out."

"really?"

"sure."

Roy lifted the lid. she looked across them all, and one caught her eye — it was red and brown, furry with long, slim, curved feathers. it reminded her of Roy — somehow simultaneously boring and colorful, standoffish but graceful. "that one."

Roy plucked it from the styrofoam, removed the price tag, and held it up for her. "that's a nice one. it's my variation of a Red Quill. i call it an 'I Love Lucy'. but it's yours now. you can call it whatever you like."

"i can just change the name?"

"don't matter. won't come when you call it." Guin chuckled; Roy even made giving a gift seem like a chore of some kind. she gently traced the long thin feathers with her finger.

the clerk moseyed back to the register with the beer. "would you quit givin them things away?"

"their mine to give if'n i want."

"except twenty percent of nothin is nothin."

"Tommy, quit your bellyachin and ring us up." Roy saw Guin pull a twenty from her belt pack. "no, now, put your money away."

"Roy, i'm getting this. let me say thank you for the gift."

Roy relented. the clerk punched the thick, worn buttons on the ancient register. "nineteen dollars and sixty-one cents."

"what?!" Roy shouted.

"nineteen dollars and sixty-one cents." Guin started to hand over the twenty, but Roy reached out and held her arm back. Guin instinctively withdrew from his touch.

"i heard you, what in the world costs so dang much?"

"RCs are a dollar'n a half, same for the Moon Pies, and six cans of beer's eleven ninety-nine."

"a six pack of Budweiser is twelve dollars??" Roy threw both his hands straight up in the air.

"what's that about?"

"i'm puttin my hands up, seein as how i'm gettin robbed."

"look, Roy, you want to drive an hour back to town to get your beer, be my guest, but if you want this beer, it's eleven ninety-nine plus tax."

Roy steamed quietly for a second, then dropped his hands. "ah, they ain't never charged what it's worth anyhow. pay the thief."

Guin laughed and handed over the twenty, and Roy grabbed their merchandise. the clerk retrieved the change and receipt and held them out to place in her hand. but Guin's free hand stayed tucked up under her sling.

"you can just put it on the counter," she said.

the clerk narrowed his eyes, but complied. "okay."

Guin picked up the coins and put it in her belt pack as Roy shuffled for the door. the clerk yelled after them.

"Roy, you want your fly money?"

"ah let it ride. i'll be back up here next weekend. keep your fingers out of it."

the clerk snickered. "okay. y'all be careful now."

for all their bickering, Roy and Tommy were obviously old friends. their bickering came from an honesty with each other they'd earned over years. Guin thought about the people in her life and realized she didn't really have any "old friends", not any that she still talked to.

the old metal passenger door creaked as Guin climbed in. Roy popped the tops off the RCs with his church key and handed one to Guin. he tossed her a Moon Pie and started up the old Ford. Guin tasted the ice cold cola, and like everything else up here, it was like being back in time. condensation rolled off the bottle across her fingers on one hand as she held the dry fly in the other. she looked at it from every angle as dappled sun landed in her lap through the filthy cracked windshield.

"my name's Guin Donnelly." Roy paused with his hand on the gear shift, a little confused. "i don't think i ever told you my full name." ah. Roy nodded.

"Roy Miller." Guin nodded. and without thinking about it, the social pressure of a handshake fell on her again, making the moment more awkward. she was pretty sure Roy felt it, too. but Roy took his hand from the gear shift and grabbed his bottle from between his legs and held it towards her. "nice to make your acquaintance, Guin Donnelly." she lifted her bottle and clinked the bottom of it to his, and they both took a sip. she relaxed, relieved. Roy gave her a little wink.

he ripped open a Moon Pie, shoving one end of it in his mouth, the plastic still around the bottom half, then put the sack with the beer behind their seats. he committed to his bite, and dry crumbs flew into the floorboard, some marshmallow clinging to his mustache. Guin admired the dry fly, its composure, the attention to tiny details, its delicate artistry. Roy stuffed the half-eaten, half-open Moon Pie in the bib pocket of his overalls and took a swig of RC. Guin held up the fly.

"i think i'll call her Little Orphan Annie."

Roy looked at her, his eyes growing large. Guin leaned away from him, a little frightened. he shouted, "LEAPIN LIZARDS!"

Guin exploded in laughter from surprise and delight.

a few sips later, they were out of the lot and headed back up to the camp site.

§

eating a Moon Pie, drinking from a glass bottle, and holding onto a dry fly while winding up the mountain road was even harder to manage with one arm in a sling. having only one hand all the time made even the most simple tasks harder. it had been nice having a buddy for the day. but tomorrow, she'd be headed back home, where there was no one. laundry, dishwasher, yardwork, cooking, changing sheets on the bed — she'd have to do it all herself. with one hand. even though her final decision was wrought out of darkness and sadness, it brought some relief knowing she'd never have to do those things ever again.

she wondered what Roy would think of her if he knew everything she was thinking, what she had decided to do. probably wouldn't make a lot of sense to him. he'd probably see it as quitting, something weak. she felt like she'd done a pretty good job of hiding it all day. but it was harder now. maybe it was her blood sugar, or just being tired. but she could feel her eyes drown, her throat prickle. she stared out the window and stuffed the breakdown back into the abyss. sunlight rippled across her face as she stared through the trees into the river below.

"you're awful quiet."

Guin said nothing.

"well. i enjoyed today."

"me, too." she watched the scenery smear by like a ruined painting. "you probably could have gone faster without me holding you up." she regretted saying it as soon as she'd said it. she was done reaching out, trying.

"yeah, probably," Roy said. the truth she already knew still stung when she heard it. "but where would the fun in that be?" that helped a little.

"so you had fun?"

"if you don't have fun fishin, quit. you can buy fish at the store if you want to eat fish."

they rode in silence for a bit.

"you comin back next year?" Roy asked.

Guin froze. he had no idea how complicated that question was. "we'll see."

"i hope you do. hell, you don't have to wait til next year. come back next weekend for all i care."

"you'd go fishing with me next weekend?"

"you're not going to get any good at it doing it once a year."

"Roy, why can't you just say, 'yes'?"

Roy chuckled. "yes i had fun, yes i'd go fishin with you next weekend. is that better?"

Guin smiled.

they pulled into the campsite. most of the others were already there. the fire was going, and they had already started cooking parts of the meal. Guin hooked her gift from Roy into the strap of her sling, the red, brown, and brass contrasting nicely against the black nylon. Roy grabbed the sack of beer and a pair of dry sneakers from behind the seat.

"my tent's the blue one if you wanna change into your dry stuff." Roy slipped out of the truck and shuffled over to some of his buddies. Guin took her bag into Roy's tent and sat on the edge of his cot. her pants were dry enough now, but she decided to change her shoes and socks. plus she could finally be alone. the sadness welled up again, and she let it slip out a little. she squeezed out a few tears, gritted her teeth, clenched her fists. she couldn't have a full on breakdown, but it felt good to relieve a little pressure, like scratching a mosquito bite even though you know you're not supposed to. after a few seconds, she took a deep breath and tamped it back down. she grabbed the hand sanitizer from her bag, slipped the bag over her shoulder, and stepped out of the tent.

she squeezed a dollop of sanitizer in her braced hand and started to rub it in with her free hand. she heard Roy's laugh. it made her smile, seeing him with his other old fart friends. he handed one of his buddies his open beer and started to undo his wader overalls. he slipped them down past his waist and sat on a stump. thick, tan Dennis went on with some story that had them laughing. she wondered if it was about one of her friends, tales of the inept womenfolk trying to learn a man's sport. Roy pushed his waders past his cargo shorts, over his knees, and... was he wearing knee pads? maybe in case he fell on the rocks. that was smart. except it was something plastic... white, hard plastic... maybe braces? he was old. it probably helped him fight the pressure of the current. as his waders crumpled to the ground, she watched, thin metal pipes below the knee pads, no socks, no skin? wait.. where were-- slowly Guin started seeing what was there, or what wasn't. Roy had no legs.

from his knees down, it was all artificial. he slipped metal "feet" from the waders and into his sneakers. he stood — awkwardly, but with no help — still listening to his buddies. they obviously were aware of what she was only now discovering, as they paid it no mind. watching him shuffle over to a nearby tree to hang up his waders, she realized his shuffle was how he had to operate the prosthetics, swinging them slightly off the ground one foot at a time. when he turned around, he saw Guin. he smiled big and waved. he reached for a beer and walked to her. by the time he was close, huge tears rolled down Guin's cheeks. she could see he noticed, as his grin softened. he looked different to her now, like a god.

"wanna beer?"

Guin was speechless. more tears.

Roy popped the beer open. "why can't you just say yes?" he said, and winked. she laughed and wiped her tears, then took a big slug of beer. "hey, slow down, enjoy that. that's one o' yer two dollar beers." she laughed again.

he walked back over to his buddies, and she followed, right on his artificial heels, like a puppy. anywhere he went for the rest of the night, she stayed right on his shoulder. the man she knew now was not the man she'd assumed that morning. she followed, safe. and he let her.

as the fish began to fry, he sat at the concrete picnic table, and she sat beside him. he felt her watching him. he didn't look at her.

"about ten years ago, i was riding our mower through the field beside our house. and i didn't know it, but a power line for a security light had been knocked down during a storm a few days earlier. i ran over the live wire, mower caught fire and exploded, and i was covered in burning gasoline." Guin sat surprised and horrified. "my son was still living with us at the time, and he ran out while i rolled around. ripped his shirt off and put me out. saved my life, thank God, but i had second and third degree burns all over. the doctors were great, but my feet and calves had what were considered 'fifth-degree' burns. i didn't even know there was such a thing. i lost all feeling, and they had to amputate to the knees. Nancy and Aaron took good care of me. i was wheelchair bound. doctor said walking again wasn't likely. and i got bored real fast. Nancy got me a fly-tyin kit that Christmas, and that gave me somethin to do while i sat for hours on end. after we did our research, i got fitted for prosthetics. and soon, with a lot of PT, i started using crutches to get around. then i got Nancy to take us on short hikes. eventually, i was able to make my way through the rocks. and then against the rapids. graduated from two crutches to one, then to a walkin stick. i'd lean on my stick with one hand and fly fish with the other. had to learn to fly fish with one hand durin all that, probably why they paired us up, you and me. after years, i was able to walk on the prosthetics alone. and now, i don't even really think about it. i think i get around better now than i did before the fire."

amazed, Guin admired Roy. "that's really incredible."

he took a sip of his beer. "ah," Roy demurred. "it just sounds that way when i tell it."

Guin laughed, not sure if that was humility or not.

saturday evening

sizzling grease dripped off breaded trout, their boiled eyes bulging white. a platter full of them sat in the center of each picnic table, with tupperware bowls and metal saucepans full of sides all around.

Guin sat next to Roy, and Sam sat next to Guin. a man named Ed offered to say grace, and everyone reached to hold hands. Guin bowed her head and pretended not to notice. Roy reached across her and grabbed Sam's hand, and they bowed their heads as well.

amen, and everyone dug in. everyone had worked up quite an appetite, and what had been a chatty social crowd became immediately quiet as everyone ate. even Dennis was more interested in dinner than telling stories. Roy made sure Guin got her catch. it was easy to find, the smallest on the plate. she and Roy shared a laugh about it, then piled on the beans and potatoes.

as plates and mess kits began to clear, the chatting resumed. soon there was laughing and more stories. Ed had a guitar and entertained with some simple country and folk tunes. some of the women talked quietly. next to Cynthia, Sam laid on a bench, her head resting on her wadded up hoodie as she listened to the music and watched the fire.

fidgeting with her brace, Guin stood at the edge of the firelight's reach, the cool darkness from the woods creeping over her back. Roy shuffled up, beer in hand, and offered her one.

"last one," he said.

"didn't we buy six?"

"well," he cracked it open, "i had three before dinner."

she took it from him, popped the top, and slurped a sip. she wasn't much for cheap beer, but it sure paired well with fish you caught yourself. Roy set down his beer and opened a pocketknife. he pulled a small, straight hickory stick from his back pocket, and started whittling. Guin watched him shave in silence for a bit.

"so, Roy. how'd you go from depressed in a wheelchair to standing in the middle of North River?"

Roy kept focused on his task. "you know, usually after dinner we talk about tv, or the weather."

Guin smiled and waited.

"well. it was a lot of years. and for most of it, i didn't ever think i'd get my life back the way i had it. it was pretty hard."

he looked up, into the fire, and she saw a flash of the darkness ripple across his face. he bit his lip and went back to his whittling.

"when i was still pretty young, i guess about ten or twelve, my granny — my mom's mom — she got some kind of cancer, went down quickly. not as much you could do for people in those days, you know. anyway, once she hit the bed, she just deteriorated so quickly. i remember several of the adults saying, 'once you stop movin, it's over.' so after the fire, as soon as i woke up, hooked up to all kinds of i dunno what all, tubes goin every which way, i can't move, can't go to the bathroom, and i see i ain't got no legs no more. well. first thing i thought was, 'once you stop movin, it's over.' and so yeah there was a lot of pain, and a lot of depression, and a lot questions and anger and loneliness and all that. and i knew i couldn't hardly count on anyone else. i was gonna have to decide to do it myself, or it weren't gettin done. and through it all i just thought, i gotta keep movin."

the darkness was gone now, and his quiet resolve had returned. nevertheless, his pithy aphorism seemed too simple, like something he'd have on a bumper sticker in the back window of his pickup. "and that did it?" Guin asked.

"did what?"

Guin realized her question, too, was simplistic. now, she wasn't sure what she was trying to ask.

"listen," Roy continued. "this ain't past tense. when i strap these things on every mornin, i gotta make that decision all over again." he gestured toward the rest of the camp. "that's why i do this."

Guin chewed on that for a bit while Roy drew another slug of beer. "you were lonely?"

"sure."

"but you had your wife. your son. you said they were there the whole time."

Roy turned to her and looked her dead in the eyes. "and i bet someone could be in a campsite full of people, and still feel lonely."

Guin thought she might be sick, having someone see through her, but she anchored her gaze to his eyes. he looked at her with that god-like look, and for what she knew was a fleeting moment, she felt like anything she told him would be received with unquestioning loyalty.

"i want to die." she couldn't bring herself to tell him the whole story. but he didn't flinch. so she continued. "i've prayed. over and over, and over. for God to take me. to kill me. to just... get me out of here. but He doesn't answer me."

Roy said, "i don't know, sounds like you got a pretty clear answer."

"how do you mean?"

"you're still here ain'tcha?"

was he right? was that God's answer? just, 'no'? that seemed like a cop out. did she just not like it because it's not the answer she wanted? and if God had really answered 'no', why?

Roy glanced across the fire, then returned to whittling. Guin followed his glance. across from them, Sam lay on the campsite bench. while Cynthia and Susan laughed and talked, Sam stared the dead stare of darkness into the heart of the fire. Guin recognized it, and now she knew Roy did, too.

the thought of Sam drowning in the same heavy bleak made Guin angry. what lifeline could she throw her? how do you save someone that's closer to the surface than you are? how do you give someone something you don't have left to give?

Guin imagined her and Sam in a cold ocean, gravity pulling them deeper. Guin sinking. Sam following. Guin kicking and pushing Sam away from her, back towards dim light, somewhere up there.

did she have one last rise in her? maybe Roy was right, in a way. maybe God had let her live this long, for Sam. if she could leave whatever she had left with Sam, it might make the approaching end that much sweeter. either way, she felt obligated.

Guin tapped Sam on the leg.

"hey. wanna go for a walk?"

Sam looked up at her, confused, but sat up. "sure."

pulling her hoodie on, Sam stood and walked toward the wooded trail. Guin looked back over her shoulder across the fire at Roy: his back to them, whittling.

§

dampness dripped from the stars. moonlight hazed through the forest canopy. pine needles squished under their feet. Guin walked slowly beside Sam. she figured she'd let her speak first. eventually she did.

"it's not that i don't want to be here. i wouldn't have come if i didn't want to be here."

Guin nodded.

"it's like... i don't want to be anywhere."

Guin understood that, but stayed quiet. she had learned this in group therapy. you listen, and let them talk, she was told. something's happening in there, so let it happen.

"i used to be angry. but. i don't have the energy left to be angry any more. it's like this big star of anger has collapsed into a black hole of hate."

after they'd walked a few steps in silence, Guin piped in, just to keep her talking. "who do you hate?"

"everyone. myself. the--" she choked up. teared up. she stopped walking. Guin stopped and looked at her. Guin watched her contort and writhe in emotional and physical pain, an empty well of tears straining to weep. finally, she caught her breath and looked at Guin. they locked eyes. it was the first time they had looked each other in the eyes. their eyes locked, the darkness lifted from Sam's face, like a veil, just for the fleeting moment. behind the veil was a young little girl, waiting for a response, looking for someone to take a chance, hoping her new friend would tell her that everything would be okay. Guin hoped her eyes offered the security that Roy's had offered her.

but Sam said nothing. she tried, her mouth open, but made no sound.

Guin waited. she felt the reflex to say, "it's okay," or to break her gaze. but Roy had caught her in this moment, by being still. Sam was falling, toward the hopeless, lonely deep. if Sam was going to find any hope, Guin had to hold on, to wait.

Sam closed her mouth and swallowed hard. the darkness cascaded down, and her eyes lost their light. Sam didn't need to say anything. Guin knew.

Guin thought back to her own trauma, the first in a long life of abuses. she told no one for years. finally, through group therapy after her divorce, she had found a place to share it, and had been received with such warmth and safety.

but it had been too late. the darkness had anchored itself. she was now hopeless, living her life alone. she had waited too long, sunk too deep to see the light above the surface. that first event had directed every course of her life from there after, every interaction with every person. every friend. every commanding officer. every man. every woman. somehow, she married. she'd hoped for a prince, her white knight, but he'd later reveal the horror inside the armor. every time he forced his hand on her, she re-lived the trauma. he was gone now. some nights she woke up, re-living it anyway. the itch under Guin's brace burned.

Sam folded up, embracing herself with one arm, scratching her elbow as a feint. Guin wished she could do something. even just get her to talk. if Sam waited too long, it might one day be too late for her, too. Sam rolled a hickory nut around with her shoe. Guin wanted to tell her it wasn't her fault, but she knew Sam wouldn't believe it right now. it took Guin years to believe it, if she did.

Sam wiped a tear with the floppy sleeve of her oversized hoodie. "out of everyone here, i think you're the most like me." Guin felt nauseous. God, please don't let that be true, Guin thought, for her sake. "when we were getting on the bus, i saw this look in your eyes, and i thought, that's how i feel. i guess that's why i've been tagging along behind you the whole trip."

they stood in silence for a while.

maybe she needs permission, Guin thought. "you don't have to tell me what's going on. but. you ought to tell someone."

Sam nodded. "i want to." the hickory nut rolled away from under Sam's shoe, and she stood motionless, staring at where it had been. "i'd like to tell you."

"okay."

"maybe... later."

"..okay."

"okay. thanks."

Guin was at a loss. she didn't know how to help. does anyone? she offered her the only comfort she thought she had. "you're not alone."

"i feel alone. all the time. i feel like no one will understand. understand what happened." Guin knew this feeling. everyone in her group felt it before opening up. but there was nothing to be done to push it. Sam would open up when she was ready. "i don't feel as alone talking to you," Sam said.

41

they locked eyes again. again, the veil of darkness peeled back, and the hurt little girl stood before Guin. Sam stared into Guin's eyes with interminable expectation.

if Guin had one last rise in her, this was it.

"i like talking to you, too," Guin said. "do you want to know what happened to me?"

Sam's gaze remained fixed, her veil still withdrawn. she shrugged. "if you want to tell me, you can."

Guin took a deep breath and spoke it all into the moonlight. their eyes locked on one another, Guin went into harrowing detail of the event that shook her life, every horrifying aftershock, the rubble left behind. she used to tremble when recounting it. she used to re-live it. but now, she was so disconnected from it, so done with it, it was like she was talking about someone else, about a book she read. there was no fixing any of it, not now. that time had long passed. as she tallied up the damage, it cemented in her mind why she'd made the decision she'd made: to kill herself.

eventually, Guin ran out of words. she thought for a second and concluded with, "so... yeah." it was only as the itch in her brace slowly returned that she noticed it had been gone.

Sam was still fixated on her. Sam breathed, seemingly for the first time since the veil lifted.

"thank you," Sam said.

this confused Guin. for what? for sharing her story? who cared. it fixed nothing for Sam. Sam hadn't even said a word yet. Guin had kicked and pushed, urging Sam back toward the surface, and Sam had only locked fingers with her. thank you? they may both sink and die.

but. Sam seemed ten pounds lighter as she sighed and started walking back toward camp. Guin followed.

"so that's it?" again, Guin felt the inadequacy of her words.

Sam turned to her. "yeah. i... thank you for telling me. that was probably hard. i'm... i can't do that yet. i can't talk about what happened to me. but i don't feel alone any more." Sam smiled. "you gave me some hope."

Guin immediately felt confusion and failure and shame. hope? she dared not tell Sam about her plans for when she got home. but even if it's a lie, better for Sam to keep believing it and have it help her for now, she reasoned. so Guin kept her shame to herself and forced a smile in return.

"really. thank you." Sam moved in for a hug.

instinctively Guin moved back.

Sam looked hurt, confused. "oh... sorry." Sam shrank.

would this undo everything that had just happened? scared, nauseous, Guin opened her arms, and Sam leaned forward and gently hugged her. even so, she couldn't bring herself to touch her with her hands, but she pressed her forearm against her back, squeezing her lightly. "thank you," Sam whispered. Guin's nausea subsided as she felt Sam's warmth. Sam let go, and they walked back to camp.

the mountain air was cool, and most of the group was around the fire, listening to Dennis spin a yarn. Sam slipped up behind Susan and Cynthia. when they heard her, they smiled big and made a spot for her on the the log bench. she glanced back at Guin and smiled, her eyes glistening in the dancing firelight.

across the firepit, Roy sat just behind everyone, facing away from them as he whittled. Guin sat on the stump next to him and watched. the limb had been whittled down to a flat sliver, with a small patch of the rough bark left on the end. he must just be doing this for fun, she thought.

"wondered where you went," Roy said.

"just for a walk."

Roy looked over at Sam. she gently wiped her bottom eyelid dry as she laughed along with the story being told around the fire.

"yeah. looks like you needed a walk." he closed his knife and pulled a fold of sandpaper from his coat pocket. he started sanding his creation.

"yeah. not sure how much good one walk does, though."

" 'the tongue has the power of life and death,' " he recited, " 'and those who love it will eat its fruit.' "

Guin nodded, and pondered. "but wait, so is it good fruit, or bad fruit?"

Roy turned to face her. "well now, that's the question, isn't it?" as she thought about it, he presented his wooden handiwork.

"beautiful." it was a flat stick.

"t'ain't for lookin at." he pushed it toward her, and she took it.

she squinted at it. "i'll call it 'hickory linguine'."

Roy sighed and took it back from her. gently, he slipped the end of it into her brace, the small piece of bark facing down. she flinched as a reflex, but then lightly gasped as she understood. she grabbed it from him, slipped it deeper into the brace, and began scratching, her eyes rolling over.

"oh wow that's good."

Roy pulled a tangerine from another coat pocket and enjoyed it while Guin enjoyed the relief. "just don't snap it off in there."

sunday

the deep blue of early morning twilight was enough to wake Guin, lightly sleeping under the cabin window. she sat up and checked her watch: about twenty minutes before her alarm would go off. she set down the watch and grabbed the hickory stick and scratched her arm to satisfaction.

it had been a good trip, better than she'd figured. but it was over, and now it was time to head home and see things through. when the time came, would she do it? would it be successful? surely. it wouldn't be hard. living was hard. this wouldn't be hard. careful not to wake anyone, she folded up her bedding.

a couple of hours later, everyone was noisily packing up their suitcases. Guin sat quietly with her bags packed, her mind on what awaited her at home.

through the open cabin window, she heard the familiar crunch of gravel and the loud creak of a hollow truck door. she was surprised to find herself smiling. she went outside to meet him.

next to his truck stood Roy in cargo shorts, his metal legs extending into his sneakers. he had two tumblers of coffee and some tangerines.

"thought you might want some breakfast."

"i think we're stopping at Waffle House on the way back."

"that's an hour from here, at least." he held out the plastic travel cup.

"i can't take your cup, Roy."

"it's Dennis's." Guin laughed and took it. Roy stabbed his thumb into a tangerine and leaned back against the truck. Guin sipped the delicious dark roast and leaned on the truck, too. "you can return it when you come back next weekend."

Guin's smile faded. she opened and closed the slide on the lid of her coffee.

"i guess it's none of my business, except you kinda made it my business when you confided in me. are you getting all the help you need?"

Guin picked the green stem from the top of her tangerine.

"are you plannin somethin?"

Guin stared at the fruit in her hand, motionless.

"what can i do?" Roy asked, a final plea.

Guin looked at him. he looked at her with interminable expectation. "i don't know," she said.

"well. thank you for being honest." Roy fished in his pocket and pulled out a thin, torn piece from the top of a donut box and held it out for her. it had his name and a telephone number. "i hope you have a counselor. or family. or a friend. but if not, please, call me. i mean it. and i really would like for you to come back this weekend."

Guin sat down her half-peeled tangerine and wiped her hand on her pants. "i'll think about it," she promised. she took it and put it in her pocket.

§

just a few more hours, and a lifetime of pain would be over. Guin stared out the window, but she wasn't looking at anything. in her mind, she was dead already. all she lacked was seeing it through.

the van pulled into the church lot. services were over, but there were a few people still inside. Susan dismissed the group, and everyone and their luggage piled out. most of these women wouldn't see each other for another year, if ever again, so everyone hugged and said, "until next time." Guin didn't hug, but smiled and said, "goodbye." Guin watched from a distance as Cynthia and Sam spoke quietly with each other for a while. they hugged, Sam wiping tears from her cheeks. Guin walked over to say goodbye to Cynthia, but Sam stopped her.

"thank you, again, for before," Sam said. "that really helped me a lot."

"oh, sure." Guin still wasn't sure how she had helped Sam. but at least she'd been able to do her final good deed.

"maybe we can stay in touch?"

"sure," Guin lied.

"i could give you my number."

Guin fished in her pocket and pulled out the box top shard with Roy's number on it. she handed it over, and Sam scratched her number on the back.

"maybe we can go walk around the art department together." she handed the torn corner back to Guin.

"maybe so."

"okay. see you soon." Sam smiled, a different person from the day before. Guin, the same, shoved the paper back into her pocket. Sam headed to her car.

meanwhile, Cynthia had gotten into a conversation with Susan, and they were walking into the church. Guin didn't care to talk to Susan and was already on the verge of tears for a thousand reasons. if she broke down in front of them, she might confess, or they might figure things out. they'd try to talk her out of it. or worse, have her checked in some place where they'd hold her for a day or more. no. better to just go on home. she walked to the car in silence and got in.

she shut the door and gripped the steering wheel hard, clenching her teeth, tamping the tears down. she wanted to see Sam soon. she wanted to say goodbye to Cynthia. but the darkness rolled over her and drowned her wants before they had time to take root. she squeezed her eyes forcing the tears to stay in place. the darkness swelled and, like a passing train, ebbed and echoed back into the abyss, for now. slowly, she opened her eyes. the church sign in front of her read, "FOLLOW ME AND I WILL YOU MAKE YOU FISHERS OF MEN"

§

golden sunlight snuck into the house through closed blinds and house plants. Guin came in with her bag and locked the door behind her. the late afternoon light dappled across everything like the campsite before the fire. she checked on her plants, sticking a finger in the soil to make sure it wasn't too dry.

she dropped her bag on the bed and unzipped it, difficult with one hand in a brace. after a couple of attempts, she took off the sling and the brace. what was the point of it any more anyway. she started taking things out of her bag, then stopped. put things away? do laundry? why?

she thought about making one last meal. but her stomach was in a knot, her appetite nonexistent. maybe just a cup of coffee. but... wouldn't that defeat the point of sleeping pills? best to just get it over with. she tossed everything on the bed into the floor. what about a note? that's something you're supposed to do, right? she'd done her will, but hadn't thought much about a note. a note to whom? her aunt? her cat?

Roy?

what could she say to him.

how could she describe

he wouldn't

--forget the note. she rolled back onto the bed, trying to get comfortable. her arm was sore from being in the sling all weekend. she stretched it and massaged it. why? why even do this, she thought. all the pain will be over soon, why bother with a small cramp.

she reached to the nightstand for the bottle and realized she didn't have any water to choke them down. she got back out of bed, bottle in hand, and headed for the bathroom. halfway to the door, she stepped on her sling, and the barb of Roy's red and brown dry fly went into the arch of her foot. she cursed loudly, and hoped Mrs. Hiddlemeyer hadn't heard. she hobbled to the bathroom and sat down on the side of the tub. she pulled out the hook, pulling the barb back through, tearing skin, with pain and blood. she didn't bother with the cut, but pried the fly from the sling. the hook was bent, and one of the long graceful feathers was broken. the body was now even more red, covered in her blood. she began crying. she wasn't sure why she was so upset, it's not like she would have been able to enjoy it in a few minutes anyway. but at a time when everything in her life either meant nothing or caused her tremendous pain, this meant something to her. it wasn't even the thing. it was that Roy respected her, and she had now disrespected him. what difference did it make, he had no way of knowing whether or not she was—

she couldn't take it any more. all of this second guessing, trying to figure things out, fighting, looking for answers, waiting... for anyone.

she felt something in her pocket digging into her leg. she pulled it out: Roy's number. she looked at it and the mangled fly. she set them both on the sink. tears dripped from her cheeks and she let them. she couldn't look at Roy's name any more, and she turned the card over: Sam's number.

she grabbed the card and threw it away in the wastebasket. she stood, taking the cup by the sink, filling it with water. she popped the top off the bottle of pills with her thumb. she held the water in one hand, the bottle in the other. she looked at the fly on the sink, broken, bloody, hurt.

monday morning

as soon as her tea kettle began to wheeze, Mrs. Hiddlemeyer removed it from the heat. the steam fogged her pop-bottle glasses as she poured her morning tea. still in curlers and her thick housecoat, she waddled down to the mailboxes. she waved at the Monday morning traffic as it rolled by — Mr. Jackson on his way to work, Mrs. Hunter taking the boys to school. she plucked out Guin's mail and started thumbing through it, weeding out the junk from the rest.

walking up Guin's driveway, she stopped to pick up a stray leaf. she tucked it in with the coupons, certain they'd all end up in the trash somewhere. underneath the cushion on the porch, she found the key to the front door and let herself inside.

she set the mail on the kitchen table, and retrieved her list from her terrycloth pocket — bring in the mail, put sheets from the dryer in the guest room, and take out the garbage in the master bathroom. she doddered into the laundry room and retrieved the sheets that were in there. she took them across the hall into the guest room and, even though she hadn't been asked to, she made the bed, pulling the comforter up tight and positioning the pillows just so. maybe there was company coming. that would be good. the young lady could probably use some company.

she knew the cat was away, but she put out some dry food and refilled the water. one less thing she'd have to do when she got back. she picked up a few stray glasses and plates and took them to the kitchen sink.

satisfied she'd done enough at the front of the house, she shuffled back toward the master bathroom. as she entered Guin's bathroom, she froze, frightened. on the floor across from her lay Guin, propped up between the tub and the commode. dried blood was caked on the sole of her foot and smeared on the tiles. her eyes were glazed over, and on the floor in front her was the pill bottle and the empty cup. Mrs. Hiddlemeyer gasped when she saw.

Guin's eyes were bloodshot, swollen, dark bags underneath. Mrs. Hiddlemeyer ran to her and dropped to her knees. Guin slowly turned her head toward her neighbor. her last remaining tears welled up, and her nose ran. in her hand, she clutched the torn card, salvaged from the trash. Mrs. Hiddlemeyer scooped up the bottle. it was empty.

"oh baby, how many did you take?"

Guin shook her head. "none. i flushed them." Mrs. Hiddlemeyer dropped the bottle and reached out to hold Guin's face in her hands. Guin was cold from laying awake on the tile all night, and her neighbor's hands were warm on her cheeks. Guin looked into her eyes, which she could really see for the first time over the top of her thick glasses. they weren't grey, but a faded blue, and they searched her, reached for her. maybe she wasn't pretending. maybe her own darkness had made her paranoid. maybe Mrs. Hiddlemeyer was genuinely kind. she felt deep remorse for everything she'd ever thought about her. Guin grabbed her hands, but not to pull them away. to feel them. to feel their warmth. to feel a kind person. she breathed in deeply, smelling the lilac of the old woman's hand soap. she exhaled, and felt lighter, warmer, brighter, as if the aged fingers could fill her with sunlight.

"what do you need, child?"

Guin squeezed the kind woman's hands, the piece of card still between her fingers.

"don't leave me."

"i'm not going to leave you, baby. i promise."

§

Guin emerged from the bedroom, freshly showered and dressed in a sharp black blazer and skirt, matching the black brace and sling. Mrs. Hiddelmeyer pushed a cup of coffee to her across the kitchen table.

"do i look presentable?"

"you are stunning, baby."

Guin sipped the coffee. until Roy, it had been a long time since someone had made her coffee. and now here it was in her own home. she embraced the warm ceramic, and the aroma helped her to stay awake. Mrs. Hiddelmeyer took dishes from the sink and put them in the dishwasher. Guin could feel the words in her throat, and the enormous urge to tamp them back down. but this was a fleeting chance she needed to take. Mrs. Hiddelmeyer shut the door of the dishwasher and sat down at the table next to Guin.

"i'm going to need a lot of help." Guin stared into Mrs. Hiddlemeyer's eyes with interminable expectation.

"i know, dear. i can only do a little bit. but i'll do what i can." Guin quivered, and her breath shallowed. "you made it this far. today, we're just gonna get through today. tomorrow can worry about itself."

Guin took a deep breath, and the quivering melted away. the peace might not last forever, but its presence meant the darkness doesn't last forever, either.

"what's this?" Mrs. Hiddelmeyer pointed to the freshly-cleaned brown and red fly affixed to Guin's lapel.

"that... is Lucy. she's a reminder. to keep moving."

Guin walked to her car, Mrs. Hiddlemeyer walking beside her.

"you want i should go with you?"

Guin looked at her neighbor's curlers and thick housecoat and stifled a laugh.

"i think i'll be okay."

"well i'll be here when you get back. i want to hear all about it, now."

Guin opened the door and tossed her résumé in the passenger seat. in her braced hand, Guin held the piece of donut box with Roy and Sam's numbers. "would you mind watching my place again this Saturday? maybe feeding the cat?"

"sure, love. i'd be happy to. going back to the mountains?"

"going to an art show with a friend."

Guin backed out of the driveway. Mrs. Hiddlemeyer waved and watched her. Guin could still see her in the rear view mirror as she drove toward town.

Guin was scared, but thankful. as she drove past homes and shops and traffic lights, her mind went back to the tree-lined river. the whole weekend churned over in her mind. the darkness. the water. the eagle. the campfire. the fish. Cynthia. Roy. Mrs. Hiddlemeyer. Sam. she thought about where she would be right now if she had given up. at the edge of every darkness, there was always a light, even if it had been hard to see. and she was thankful.

Guin parked her car in the shade of a gently swaying poplar. she got out, straightened her skirt, and stepped from the shade, résumé tucked under her sling. it was summer, and the sun was hot on her cheeks. she breathed in the warm breeze, and Lucy's feathers danced. the light rolled over her. she walked taller. her stride lengthened. she felt her body relax, even her face. she might have even grinned. she was moving. she was alive.

she stepped through the glass doors, and a man in a suit rose to meet her.

"are you Guin? Kathleen's friend?" he walked toward her.

"yes," she said, "and i'm really looking forward to this."

she smiled at him and extended her hand.

※   ※   ※

NATIONAL

SUICIDE

PREVENTION

LIFELINE

™

1-800-273-TALK (8255)

suicidepreventionlifeline.org

National Suicide Prevention Lifeline

the **National Suicide Prevention Lifeline — 1.800.273.TALK (8255)** — is FREE, confidential, and always available. help a loved one, a friend, or yourself. Lifeline calls are directed to a crisis center in your community to better direct you to the people who can help you most.

suicide warning signs

these signs may mean someone is at risk for suicide. risk is greater if a behavior is new or has increased and if it seems related to a painful event, loss, or change.

- talking about wanting to die or to kill oneself.
- looking for a way to kill oneself, such as searching online or buying a gun.
- increasing the use of alcohol or drugs.
- acting anxious or agitated; behaving recklessly.

- sleeping too little or too much.
- withdrawing or feeling isolated.
- talking about feeling hopeless or having no reason to live.
- talking about feeling trapped or in unbearable pain.
- talking about being a burden to others.
- showing rage or talking about seeking revenge.
- displaying extreme mood swings.

SUICIDE IS PREVENTABLE.

call the Lifeline at 1.800.273.TALK (8255).

with help comes hope.

about the author

paul andrew skidmore is a believer, follower, and filmmaker in Tennessee.

if you enjoyed this story, you might also enjoy a cup of coffee with its author. he'd likely enjoy it, too.

skidmorep.com/books
facebook.com/parabolosbooks
twitter.com/skidmorep

Made in the USA
Monee, IL
10 June 2021

70849416R00049